NO LONGER PROPERTY OF
SEATTLE PUBLIC LIBRARY

Red Spider Hero

enchantedlionbooks.com

This book has been set in Bembo, an old-style humanist serif typeface originally cut by Francesco Griffo
in 1495 and revived by Stanley Morison in 1929.

First edition published in the United States in 2015 by Enchanted Lion Books, 351 Van Brunt Street, Brooklyn, NY 11231
Copyright © 2015 Enchanted Lion Books
Text copyright © 2015 by John Miller
Illustrations copyright © 2015 by the family of Giuliano Cucco
Photo of "spider on sidewalk" is Copyright © by Jeff Rogerson 2015
Photo of "spider on flower" is Copyright © by Steven Begin 2015
All rights reserved under International and Pan-American Copyright Conventions. A CIP record is on file with the Library of Congress
ISBN: 978-1-59270-176-6
Printed and bound in August 2015 by RR Donnelley Asia Printing Solutions Limited
Design and layout by Sarah Klinger
1 3 5 7 9 10 8 6 4 2
First Edition

Red Spider Hero

Story by
John Miller

Illustrations by
Giuliano Cucco

ENCHANTED LION BOOKS
NEW YORK

On a small patch of sidewalk, there once lived many teeny, tiny red spiders.

These red spiders were so small that when it rained, they never got wet. And when people stepped on them, they never got squashed.

They enjoyed the many advantages of being so tiny, and all of the spiders were quite content.

All, that is, except for a lively little spider named Harry.

One day, Harry began to stamp his feet and yell and carry on in such a way that everyone gathered around to see what was the matter.

"I'm tired of being a little spider on a small patch of sidewalk!" Harry hollered. "I want to see the world! So I've made up my mind to run away and become the most famous spider to have ever lived."

While Harry hollered, his grandfather, who had been listening, came forward.

"If you want to run away, go right ahead, Harry. But it will take you more than a week to reach the end of the sidewalk, and a whole year of climbing through grass to cross the park."

Harry was not easily discouraged, so he thought for a moment and said to his grandfather, "Then I'll build a boat, and the next time it rains I'll sail down a river of raindrops to the ocean. I'll cross the ocean, and there I'll discover a new land that no one has ever explored before."

"From there, I will go deep into the jungle. I will become a famous hunter and explorer, and everyone will know me throughout the world."

"That sounds very exciting, Harry," said his wise old grandfather, "but from what I've heard about hunters and explorers, they face many risks."

"Well, maybe they do," said Harry.

He thought about all of the ferocious animals in the jungle, with their horns, claws, poisonous fangs, and spooky eyes. And how they would chase after him and gobble him up.

Harry considered for a moment.

"Well," he slowly replied, "before any one can catch me, a flea will hop by and I'll jump on its back and gallop far away."

"We'll join a flea circus and I'll march in the circus parade. I'll become a famous flea rider and tour all over the country. Word will spread far and wide, and I'll be known throughout the whole world."

"That sounds like a daring adventure, Harry," said his grandfather, "but as we know, fleas like to eat little red spiders."

"Well, maybe they do," said Harry.

He suddenly thought of what would happen if the fleas got hungry. He could see them bucking him off their backs and chasing him out of the circus tent, coming closer and closer with their big, angry teeth.

Again Harry considered for a moment.

"Well, just as the fleas are about to catch me," he answered, "I'll climb up a dandelion stalk, grab onto some dandelion seeds, and fly off with the wind."

"I'll fly up and up and become the first red spider to circle the earth. And when I look down, I will see everyone looking up at me with binoculars and telescopes as I pass by. They will wave to me and I'll wave back, and everybody will know me throughout the world."

"But from what I know about dandelion seeds," said his grandfather, "there are many that never return to earth."

"Maybe that's so," said Harry.

He imagined himself all alone, with no friends to play with, and the dandelion seeds rising higher and higher. He saw himself yelling for help, but no one could see or hear him anymore. Not even with the most powerful telescope.

"Well, I will just have to jump onto the back of a dragonfly, and we will fly away together."

"Where will you go?" asked his grandfather.

"I don't know..."

"Back to the jungle?"

"Oh no!" cried Harry.

"Back to the flea circus?"

"Never!"

"Maybe the dragonfly will bring you back home?"

"Maybe..."

Harry thought, and then he thought some more.

"Yes," he said at last, "that's what I will do.
I will ask the dragonfly to bring me home, where
everyone on our sidewalk will be waiting for me.
I will walk down Main Street, escorted by the
mayor himself. A big brass band will be playing
and flags will be flying!"

"I will walk up to you and you will shake my hand and say, 'Now that you have become famous the world over, it is indeed our pleasure to welcome you home.'"

Harry's wise old grandfather proudly shook each of Harry's four hands. "Welcome back to our sidewalk, Red Spider Hero!"

"It's tiring being so famous," Harry sighed. "Now I must rest and play with my friends again."

"Very well," nodded his grandfather. "Go off and play, but don't be late for supper."

With that, Harry dashed off down
the sidewalk, brimming with excitement
over his adventures and the games he was
about to play.

Red Spider Mites

Real red spiders, or spider mites, are smaller than the head of a pin. If it weren't for their bright scarlet color, you would never notice them. Their color warns predators, such as ladybugs or ground-feeding birds, not to eat them. Any bird or bug that does is left with such a terrible taste in its mouth that it never forgets the experience or the spider's color.

Although red spiders have eight legs like other spiders, scientists classify them as mites, of which there are around 1,200 species. You can find red spider mites on the underside of leaves or crawling on rocks, walls, and pavement.

Children, who have better eyesight for tiny things than adults, are good at spotting them.